Emma
and
Julia
Love Ballet

Barbara McClintock

Scholastic Press • New York

*E*mma wakes up early.

Julia wakes up early, too.

Emma has breakfast.

Julia has breakfast, too.

They both get dressed.

They both have ballet lessons
this morning.

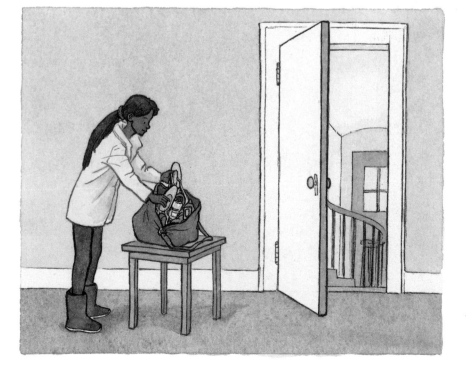

Emma's mother drives her to her lesson.

Julia takes the bus by herself.

When Emma gets to the dance studio, she puts away her coat and bag.

Julia does the same.

Emma's teacher begins class.

Julia's teacher begins class, too.

Emma loves her teacher.

Julia is devoted to her teacher.
Both teachers make them work very, very hard.

They stretch and move until their muscles are warm.

Emma and Julia love ballet.

Some of Emma's friends take tap lessons.

Some of Julia's friends take tap, too.

Some of Emma's friends take jazz lessons.

Some of Julia's friends take jazz, too.

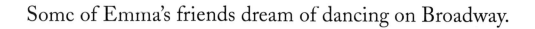

Some of Emma's friends dream of dancing on Broadway.

Some of Julia's friends *are* dancing on Broadway.

But Emma and Julia love ballet.

After class is done, Emma says good-bye to her teacher.

Emma's parents are waiting to take her home.
She is excited about the performance they
are going to see tonight in the city!

Julia is *in* the performance tonight!

She and the other dancers stay to rehearse.
They make sure all the steps and movements are perfect.

Late in the afternoon, Emma and her family make dinner together.

Julia has a snack with the other dancers.

Emma does her homework.

Julia reads a book.

Soon it's time to go.
Emma wears her best dress.

She puts on her fancy coat.

Emma and her family drive to the city.

Julia puts her toe shoes on again.

She and the other dancers warm up.

As Emma and her family arrive at the theater . . .

. . . Julia and the other dancers finish warming up onstage.
Now it's time to go downstairs to get into their costumes.

Emma takes a program and finds her seat.

Julia puts on makeup.

Emma reads every word in her program.
Then she reads it all over again. She is very excited.

Julia waits in the wings for the curtain to go up.
She is very excited, too!

The theater lights dim. The music begins. The curtain rises.
The dancers glide onstage. Gracefully they bend, and swirl, and leap.

Emma watches every move.
She can feel every lift of the dancers' arms, every step and pause.

Julia leaps,

spins,

and balances on her toes.

She feels like her heart is flying.
Emma's heart is flying, too.

When the ballet ends, the audience applauds and cheers.
Julia and the other dancers bow. The curtain goes down, and the lights go on.

Emma's parents take her backstage.
She sees Julia in her costume.
Emma's heart is pounding.

"Would you sign my program, please?"
asks Emma.

"I'd love to!" says Julia.

"Someday," Emma tells Julia,
"I will dance onstage—just like you!"

Julia gives Emma a big hug. "And once
I dreamed of being a dancer—just like *you*!"

Emma and Julia love ballet.

To Kathleen with love

I am grateful to my sister, Kathleen, who loved ballet and who took me to my first professional performance to see the magnificent Judith Jamison. And I'm thankful to Ms. Jamison, who made me love the world of dance in all of its forms. From the moment she stepped onto the stage, she transformed time and space. She created shapes and moved with such authority, grace, and strength that it stunned me. I've never forgotten that performance. What a phenomenal privilege to have had this as my introduction!

I would also like to thank the Connecticut Concert Ballet for allowing me to sketch and photograph classes at their school, and a special thanks to the Meikles for all their help.

—B. McC.

All rights reserved. Published by Scholastic Press, an imprint of Scholastic Inc., *Publishers since 1920.*
SCHOLASTIC, SCHOLASTIC PRESS, and associated logos are trademarks and/or registered trademarks of Scholastic Inc.

The publisher does not have any control over and does not assume any responsibility for author
or third-party websites or their content.

Library of Congress Cataloging-in-Publication Data
McClintock, Barbara, author, illustrator.
Emma and Julia love ballet / Barbara McClintock. — First edition.   pages cm
Summary: A story that follows the everyday life of two dancers, one a professional ballerina, the other
a very young student, both of whom love ballet.
ISBN 978-0-439-89401-2 (hardcover : alk. paper)
1. Ballet dancers—Juvenile fiction. 2. Ballet—Juvenile fiction. 3. Dance recitals—Juvenile fiction. [1. Ballet dancing—
Fiction. 2. Ballet—Fiction.] I. Title.   PZ7.M47841418Em 2016   [E]—dc23   2014026920
10 9 8 7 6   20 21 22 23 24
Printed in China 38   First edition, March 2016

The text type was set in Adobe Caslon.
The display type was set in Harman.
Barbara McClintock used a dip pen and India ink, Winsor Newton
watercolors, and gouache to create the art for this book.
Book design by Leslie Mechanic